MRS. DUNPHY'S DOG

MRS. DUNPHY'S DOG

BY CATHARINE O'NEILL

VIKING KESTREL

VIKING KESTREL
Viking Penguin Inc., 40 West 23rd Street, New York, New York 10010, U.S.A.
Penguin Books Ltd, Harmondsworth, Middlesex, England
Penguin Books Australia Ltd, Ringwood, Victoria, Australia
Penguin Books Canada Limited, 2801 John Street, Markham, Ontario, Canada L3R 1B4
Penguin Books (N.Z.) Ltd, 182–190 Wairau Road, Auckland 10, New Zealand

First published in 1987 by Viking Penguin Inc.
Published simultaneously in Canada
Printed in Japan by Dai Nippon Printing Co. Ltd.
Set in Cloister Old Style
3 5 7 9 10 8 6 4 2

Library of Congress Cataloging in Publication Data
O'Neill, Catharine. Mrs. Dunphy's dog.
Summary: Mrs. Dunphy's dog discovers that he can read.
[1. Dogs—Fiction. 2. Reading—Fiction] I. Title.
PZ7.0554Mr 1987 [E] 86-15729 ISBN 0-670-81135-1

For my mother

James was Mrs. Dunphy's dog and they were very happy together. Every afternoon they would ramble in the park. And every evening they would stroll to the newsstand to pick up Mrs. Dunphy's paper.

Back at home, Mrs. Dunphy sat in the big rose chair with a cup of tea and a tart. She ate up the news, cover to cover.

James always sat beside her, looking for crumbs.

Whenever Mrs. Dunphy found a good animal story, she read it out loud.

James didn't pay any attention.

When Mrs. Dunphy had finished reading, she usually fell asleep. By and by, the paper drifted to the floor. Then James ripped it to smithereens.

But one evening, as James began to demolish the news, a photo caught his eye. James stopped and stared hard. Then he made out these words:

GIANT FLYING CAT TERRIFIES TOTS

It was the first thing James had ever read. He didn't know how he'd done it. It was all he could do for that evening.

The next evening, when the paper landed, James scratched, scrunched his snout, and read this story top to bottom:

TEN-YEAR-OLD GIRL RAISED BY PIGS

James studied Mrs. Dunphy. She must be awfully intelligent. After all, she'd been reading papers for as many years as he'd been tearing them up.

Soon James was intelligent, too. He took easily to reading and learned many fine things:

WOMAN BECOMES HUMAN MOUSETRAP

BOY TRADES SISTER FOR BIKE

DOOMED MAN TAKES MAIL TO WORLD BEYOND

Alas, it was no good talking to Mrs. Dunphy. He tried to tell her about the pumpkins from outer space.

She only looked silly and scratched him harder behind the ears. Still, James kept reading.

Soon James was all bottled up with news. One night he didn't sleep at all thinking about the ice cream man who turned into a Gila monster.

Waiting all day for the paper was almost more than James could bear. So one afternoon he set off for the newsstand by himself.

Blissfully, James browsed through the headlines. He didn't notice the newsman's cat until it sat up and yawned.

Well, thought James, here's my chance to talk about the news. Out popped the story of the amazing flying cat.

"Ridiculous," snapped the newsman's cat. "You couldn't get a kitty off the ground for all the mice in China."

James was startled. The cat didn't believe his story. James decided the cat was a bit of a crank.

It began raining as James hurried back to Mrs. Dunphy in the park. James spied a rabbit near Mrs. Dunphy's bench. He crouched down and blurted out the incredible story of the monster bunny.

"Impossible," answered the rabbit. "I've yet to see a bunny bigger than a breadbox. Trust a dog to fall for a tale like that!"

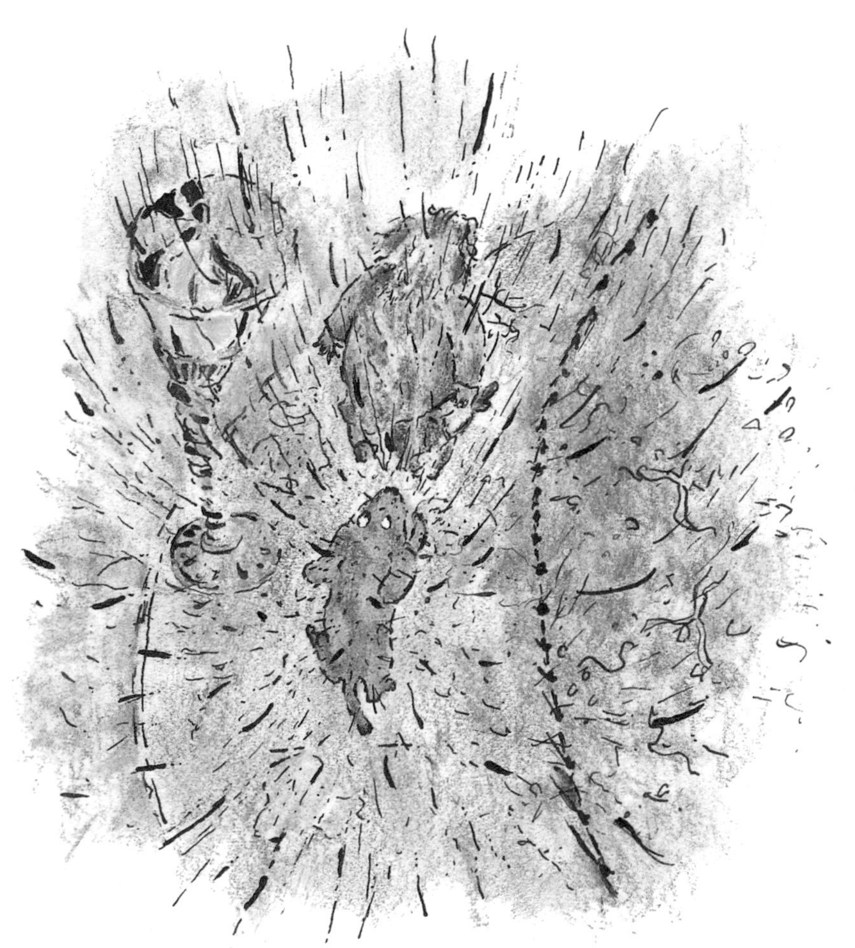

The rain pounded down. James and Mrs. Dunphy ran home, but James felt very sad. He was beginning to think that the stories were not absolutely true.

When Mrs. Dunphy sat down to read, James stayed in the kitchen. A mouse tiptoed out to wuffle up tart crumbs. James didn't say a word about the mousetrap woman.

The next evening James ignored the paper altogether. Mrs. Dunphy grew worried. She searched the news and read him all the best stories she could find.

James just stared out the window.

It wasn't long before Mrs. Dunphy fell asleep. James decided to skip the paper and sink his teeth into a good book. He knocked one off the shelf and set to work. Then a picture caught his eye.

Curious, James nudged the book open with his nose.

Well. It turned out to be awfully good. The book's name was *Peter Pan*. The dog, Nana, was terribly brave.

The next evening, James got out another book. The people were nice but the dog was top-notch, bold as a lion and with a fine sense of humor, too.

It wasn't long before James discovered *Lassie Come Home*. He wept buckets and used up all Mrs. Dunphy's best handkerchiefs.

Mrs. Dunphy didn't mind putting books back on the shelf. James had almost knocked off her entire collection. But he wasn't worried. There was a library right down the street.

James and Mrs. Dunphy still walk to the newsstand every evening to pick up the paper.

And every evening Mrs. Dunphy settles into the big rose chair with a cup of tea and a tart. She reads the paper, cover to cover. James sits right beside her, looking for crumbs and reading a good, big book.

But sometimes Mrs. Dunphy falls asleep and the paper slides to the floor. Then James looks up to see a story so astonishing it makes his teeth tickle.

And even though James is an intelligent dog…

he drops what he's doing and eats up every word.